THE CASE OF THE
RECURRING
STOMACHACHES

by Howard J. Bennett, MD

illustrated by Spike Gerrell

MAGINATION PRESS

WASHINGTON, DC

American Psychological Association

For Dana and Katie. Also, I would like to thank
Benny Kerzner, MD and Stacie Isenberg, PsyD
for their help with the manuscript—HJB

For Milly B and for the 11-year-old version of myself.
And for Max Archer, for helping me understand just why I'm an illustrator—SG

Published by
MAGINATION PRESS
An Educational Publishing Foundation Book
American Psychological Association
750 First Street, NE
Washington, DC 20002

The information in this book is not a substitute for medical advice nor is it intended to replace the medical advice you receive from your physician.

For more information about our books, including a complete catalog, please write to us, call 1-800-374-2721, or visit our website at www.apa.org/pubs/magination.

Book design by Sandra Kimbell
Printed by Worzalla, Stevens Point, Wisconsin

Library of Congress Cataloging-in-Publication Data

Bennett, Howard J.
  Max Archer, kid detective : the case of the recurring stomachaches / by Howard J. Bennett ; illustrated by Spike Gerrell.
     p. cm.
  "American Psychological Association."
  Summary: "Information and tools to tackle recurring stomach aches in children caused commonly by lactose intolerance, constipation, or stress. Resource material at the end includes cognitive behavioral techniques for dealing with stress, bonus activities (jokes or puzzles), as well psycho-educational information suitable for parents"--Provided by publisher.
  ISBN 978-1-4338-1129-6 (pbk. : alk. paper) -- ISBN 978-1-4338-1130-2 (hardcover : alk. paper)
  1. Stomach--Diseases--Juvenile literature. 2. Stomach--Diseases--Psychological aspects--Juvenile literature. I. Gerrell, Spike, ill. II. Title. III. Title: Case of the recurring stomachaches.
  RC817.B46 2012
  616.3'3--dc23
                                    2011040292

Manufactured in the United States of America

10 9 8 7 6 5 4 3 2 1

Contents

CHAPTER 1

CALL ME MAX

My name is Max.

Max Archer.

I'm a kid detective.

That means I help kids

with their problems.

But I'm not just a kid detective.
I'm also a kid. That means I go to school and
play sports like everyone else.

But after my homework and chores are done,
my office door is always open.

C U THEN

I was reading *Harry Potter and the Chamber of Secrets* (for the fifth time) when I got a text message from a girl named Emily Banks.

Hi Max. I got your number from my neighbor, Billy Parker. I need to see you right away.

Billy Parker is an 8-year-old who used to wet the bed. He was my last case.

I texted her back.

No problem. I have to walk my dogs, but I can meet with you at my office at 5.

Three seconds later, I got another text.

c u then.

One of the cool things about being a kid detective is that I never know what I'll be working on. Like the time I had to figure out why Matt McCreery wouldn't go on sleepovers. It turned out he sucked his thumb at night and was embarrassed someone would find out—including me. Once he opened up, I helped him solve the problem in a few weeks.

CHAPTER 3

EYES ON the PRIZE

Emily knocked on my door at five o'clock sharp.

"Door's open," I said.

Emily opened the door and peeked inside.

"Hi, Max," she said.

"Hi, Emily," I said.

Emily stood there like she was waiting for the school nurse to show up with a spoonful of icky-tasting medicine. I motioned for her to sit down. Then I asked her if she wanted a glass of OJ or a cup of hot chocolate.

"I'd like some orange juice, please," she said.

I could tell right away that Emily was very polite.

She was so nervous that she was twisting the bottom of her T-shirt into a knot. I prefer the direct approach with clients, so I dove right in.

"How can I help?" I said.

"I get stomachaches a lot, and sometimes I pass gas," said Emily with a pink flush to her cheeks.

Boys don't mind telling me if they're gassy. In fact, they're usually proud of it! But girls get embarrassed talking about farts, poop, and other icky stuff.

"Have you seen a doctor?" I said.

"I saw my doctor a few weeks ago. He said everything was normal. But I still get stomachaches. My parents thought you might be able to help."

"That's what I'm here for," I said. "How often do you get stomachaches?"

"Once or twice a week," said Emily.

"Do you have to stop when the pain comes or can you continue doing stuff like it wasn't even there?"

"I mostly keep doing things," said Emily. "But sometimes I have to sit down."

"Okay, that's a start. For the next week, I want you to keep track of when you eat and poop and what your poops look like."

"You want me to look at my poops? That's gross, Max!"

"Actually, your parents are the ones that have to look at your poops."

"What? My parents? Ick!"

"Parents know more about poop than kids, so we need them to find out if yours are hard or big enough to cause stomachaches. If you're embarrassed having them look at your poop, they can check after you leave the bathroom."

"All right, Max. You're the boss."

"Text me when you're ready to meet again," I said.

CHAPTER 4

The usual suspects

Emily sent me a text message the following week. I was studying the eating habits of my Indian stick insect when my phone buzzed.

Hi, Max. I'm done with my chart. Can we meet today?

I put down my magnifying glass and texted her back.

You bet. Can you be at my office at 5:30?

c u then.

Emily knocked on the door at five-thirty on the nose.

"Door's open," I said.

Emily marched in and sat on my chair.

"OJ?" I said.

"I'd love some," she said.

Emily took the poop chart out of her backpack and put it on the desk.

"Here it is, Max. What do you think?"

"The first thing I look for is a connection between eating, pooping, and pain."

"How come?" said Emily.

"Because poop and milk products are common reasons kids have stomachaches. Have you learned about digestion in school?"

"A little."

"Digestion takes place in the stomach and small intestine. The body uses chemicals and lots of water to turn food into tiny particles that can be absorbed into the bloodstream. The food that can't be digested comes out as poop, but the waste that's left over at the end of the small intestine is very watery. The body has to reabsorb the excess water to keep us healthy."

"How?" said Emily.

"As the liquid waste moves through the large intestine, more and more water is absorbed until you have formed a poop at the end."

"How does the waste get through the large intestine?" said Emily.

"Ah, that's the million-dollar question! Have you ever heard of peristalsis?"

"No," said Emily.

"Peristalsis is the word that describes how the intestinal tract moves things from one end to the other. The muscles in the intestine squeeze and relax in an orderly fashion to push things along. If a person has big or hard poops, the large intestine has to work a lot harder to keep things moving and that can cause stomachaches."

Emily and I looked at her poop chart and saw that she had soft, easy-to-pass poops twice a day.

"What does this mean?" she said.

"It means poop is not causing your stomachaches."

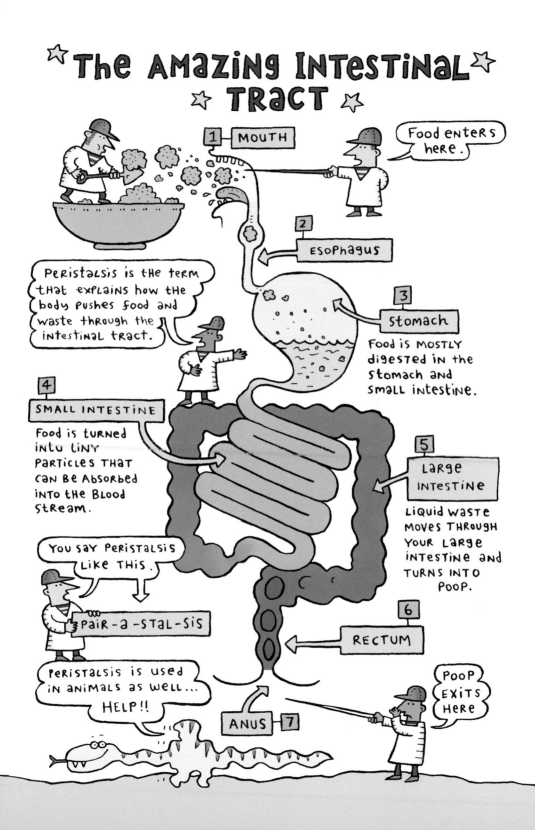

CHAPTER 5

The MiLK LiNK

"Okay, Max. So this means we can cross one suspect off the list. What's next?"

"Have you ever heard of lactose? It's the fancy name for milk sugar. Lactose is in all products made from cow's milk."

"Can lactose cause stomachaches?" said Emily.

"Lactose is supposed to be digested in your small intestine. But if you don't make the chemical that's needed to carry out this task, it ends up in your large intestine."

"And that's a problem?" said Emily.

"You bet. If lactose gets into your large intestine, the bacteria that live there digest it for you. Unfortunately, this process can cause nausea, stomachache, gas, and loose poops. It's called being *lactose intolerant.* Some people with lactose intolerance feel bad thirty minutes after they ingest lactose. Others may not notice anything for a few hours."

Bacteria are so small you can't see them without a microscope.

There are more bacteria living in your large intestine than there are humans on earth.

"Is that why people don't always know that lactose is causing their problem?"

"Yep."

"How can I tell if lactose is causing my stomachaches?" said Emily.

"The easiest way to find out is to not drink milk and to stop eating yogurt, cheese, and ice cream for a week and see what happens."

"And if the pain goes away, we've figured it out?"

"Bingo!" I said. "So what's our next step?"

"To go a week without milk products," said Emily.

"Tell your mom and dad about the plan and meet me back here in one week."

Emily had already taken out her cell phone and was texting her mom.

"I'm on it," she said. "See you next week."

CHAPTER 6

same place, different time

The following week, I was in my office playing
Plants vs. Zombies when I heard a knock on the door.

"Door's open," I said.

Emily came in quietly and sat down. She was twisting her
shirt big-time, so I knew we had a problem.

"I've been off milk products all week, but I'm still having
stomachaches," she said glumly.

"Sorry, Em, but being a detective is hard work. You don't
score a goal every time you kick a soccer ball."

"What do you mean?" said Emily.

"This week was a test to see if milk products were causing
your stomachaches. Now we know they aren't. So that's
another suspect we can cross off our list."

"I see," she said. "It's like finding out someone didn't commit a crime in a mystery. You still don't know who did it, but the list of possibilities has gotten smaller."

"Exactly," I said. "Do you like mysteries?"

"No, but my dad does. Sometimes he tells me about the books he's reading."

"I love mysteries," I said.

"What do we do now?" said Emily.

"We look at the next suspect on our list—stress."

"Stress? How does stress cause stomachaches?"

"To solve that mystery, we have to look at something called the mind-body connection."

MiNd oVeR MaTTeR

"Have you ever heard of the *fight versus flight response?*"

"I think so," said Emily. "Isn't that when a person has to decide if he should run or fight if he's being threatened by a wild animal?"

"That's right. And in a split second, the non-thinking part of your brain makes your body respond to the threat in ways that increase strength, improve vision, and make your heart beat really fast so you can fight back or run away. The thoughts and actions of your mind and body are connected."

"What does this have to do with stomachaches?" she said.

"Nowadays most people don't have to worry about being eaten by lions or tigers. Instead, threats usually come from stressful situations at home and school."

"Like worrying about doing well on a test?"

"Or getting bullied. But lots of times, kids may not be aware of the stressful situations they're dealing with."

"I see," said Emily. "My brother says my stomachaches aren't real. One time, he even told my parents I was making them up."

"The pains are very real, Emily. But the same actions that would give you extra strength if a lion is chasing you can cause stomachaches or headaches when you're challenged with day-to-day stress. The nerves in your intestinal tract overreact to the normal process of digesting food and pushing waste out of your body."

"And that's what causes the pain?" she said.

"Exactly."

"But I like school."

"I know you do, so here's an assignment that can help. Think about everything we've discussed, including what might be bothering you and things you worry about. It would also help if you talk to your mom and dad. Let's see if we can make a connection."

"Okay," she said. "If stress is the next suspect on the list, I'm ready to go."

"Excellent," I said. "Same time next week?"

"You bet."

CHAPTER 8

STRESS BUSTERS

Emily texted me six days after our last meeting. I was doing science homework when the message came in.

Hi, Max. I think I have some answers. Can't wait to c u tomorrow.

I texted her back.

Me too.

When Emily arrived the following afternoon, she came into the office with a calm determination on her face.

"It was like you said, Max. I couldn't think of anything stressful until I talked with my mom. She said that I worry about being called on in class and that I like everything to be perfect. She also pointed out that I tie my shirts in knots when I'm nervous."

I guess I wasn't the only one who noticed Emily's clothes took a beating!

"I'm glad she was helpful," I said.

"But how come the stomachaches don't happen when I feel stressed?"

"Do you remember what I said about lactose? That some people feel bad right after they drink milk, but others don't feel anything for hours?"

"Yes! So my stomachaches don't have to happen at the exact moment I'm feeling nervous?"

"Exactly. Stress is a part of everyone's life to some degree, but how and when people deal with it varies. Some people get angry or moody, while others get headaches, stomachaches, or loose poops. Some people feel bad when they anticipate what's going to happen, while others feel bad after the stress is over."

"Wow, Max, this is so helpful. I didn't realize stress could be such a pain in the neck."

"Or stomach," I said. "Can you think of other ways kids might be stressed?"

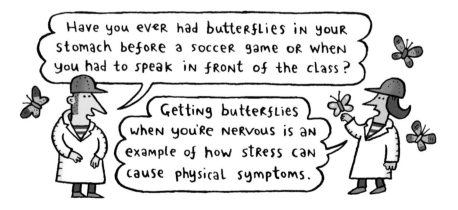

"Let's see," said Emily. "I guess it could come from your parents or teachers, or if you have trouble with a subject like math."

"Good examples," I said. "But the stress doesn't even have to be about schoolwork. It could happen if you're not getting along with your friends or your classmates are trying to exclude you from what they're doing. It could also happen because a close relative is really sick or your parents are arguing a lot."

"Gosh, Max. The mind-body connection is tricky. So what can I do?"

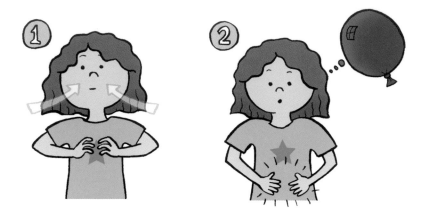

"You use the thinking part of your brain to take control of the non-thinking part with a super-duper system I call Stress Busters. That way, you can get your mind-body connection working for you!"

"The first step in busting stress is to learn to turn off your *fight versus flight response.* You start the calming process by taking deep breaths. Here's how.

1. With your mouth closed, breathe in very slowly through your nose.

2. Imagine you are trying to blow up a balloon that is in the lower part of your belly.

3. Feel your belly rise as you breathe in.

4. Keep inhaling until you can't anymore. Hold your breath for one or two seconds.

5. Very slowly, let the air out through your lips as though you were breathing through a straw. Keep exhaling until it feels like there is no air left in your body.

6. Repeat the breathing exercise five or ten times."

"OK," said Emily. "I can do that."

"Great. I have a few more tricks up my sleeve that can help tame stress. The next time you get a stomachache, think of it as a hideous monster that's trying to push you around."

"I will run him off with my sword!" said Emily.

"Or imagine the stomachache is coming from an evil ogre who's attacking you with an electric pain machine."

"I will turn down the pain switch with my amazing mind!" said Emily.

"Awesome," I said. "But the last trick is the best. If you imagine yourself responding to a stressful situation in a way you would hope to react, then when you actually face that situation, your reaction can be just what you practiced."

"No way," said Emily.

"Way!" I said. "Remember that you told me you worry about being called on in class?"

"Yes," said Emily.

"Close your eyes and imagine that your teacher asked you to read a poem out loud. You recite the poem skillfully and when you're done, she says *Great job, Emily. Your delivery was wonderful.* As you imagine this, can you see yourself feeling happy and relaxed?"

"I can!" said Emily.

"So the next time you get stressed about something at school, remember that you can use your imagination to control the situation."

"Wow, Max. This mind-body stuff is pretty cool."

"It sure is."

"But what if the Stress Busters don't work?"

"It can take time to learn a new skill so don't give up if it doesn't work right away. And if the pains continue like before, the next step would be to see a psychologist or another type of talking doctor. They are experts at helping kids understand what's bothering them and figuring out ways to control the problem."

"Thanks, Max. This is really helpful."

"You're welcome, Em. Send me a text to let me know how things are going."

"You bet."

CHAPTER 9
I'M the BOSS OF MY BODY

I got a text from Emily two months later. This is what it said.

Hi, Max. My parents have been great, and the Stress Busters definitely helped. I saw a really nice psychologist who taught me other ways to take charge of my body. I still love school, and I hardly get stomachaches anymore.

I texted her back.

Way to go, Emily. You're a star!

extra activities and information

How to Tame Your Stress Monster

by Max

This may sound surprising, but everyone has to deal with stress. If you were an animal, stress would come from having to find your next meal or avoid becoming one. Fortunately, Mother Nature has provided animals with the tools they need to fight or protect themselves depending on which strategy is most likely to succeed. This process, called the *fight versus flight response*, happens automatically and is controlled by the "non-thinking" part of the brain.

Although people don't have to worry about being eaten by predators, they still encounter situations that require the fight versus flight response. If a small child wanders into the street, his mom or dad has to run full speed to make sure a car doesn't hit him. But most of the time, people deal with stress that is less urgent. Parents worry about paying bills. Kids worry about school. Detectives worry if anyone will need them to solve a case!

These kinds of worries trigger a variation of the fight versus flight response that is less intense, but can last for longer periods

of time. When it happens, you may experience the following
symptoms:

- rapid heart rate
- feeling tense, nervous or queasy
  (like you're going to throw up)
- sweaty body, especially your palms and the soles
  of your feet
- stomachache
- headache

In addition to making you worry, stress can make you feel sick.
When that happens, you have a Stress Monster that is trying to
push you around. Here are some ways to defeat it.

STEP 1: Turn Off the Fight Versus Flight Response
Because there is no threat or animal that wants to eat you, you don't
need your body to get ready for a fight. Your heart doesn't need to
speed up and your muscles don't need to tense. You can turn off the
response by helping your body calm down.

Start the calming process by taking deep breaths.

- With your mouth closed, breathe in very slowly
  through your nose.
- Imagine you are trying to blow up a balloon that
  is in the lower part of your belly.
- Feel your belly rise as you breathe in.
- Keep inhaling until you can't anymore.
- Hold your breath for one or two seconds.
- Very slowly, let the air out through your lips as though you were
  breathing through a straw.
- Keep exhaling until it feels like there is no air left in your body.
- Don't breathe for one or two seconds.
- Repeat the breathing exercise five or ten times.

The first time you practice the breathing exercise, do it while you
are lying down on the floor or your bed. Put a small book on your

lower abdomen. If you are breathing correctly, the book will rise when you inhale and lower when you exhale. Once you learn the technique, you do not need to use a book.

Continue the calming process by relaxing your muscles. Do this by tensing them as hard as you can and then releasing them. At  first, tense your muscles for a couple of seconds before relaxing. As you get better at this, challenge yourself by tensing them for longer periods of time. You can do it seated, standing or lying down.

- Tense your face muscles by squeezing your eyes shut.
- Raise your shoulders like you were trying to get them to touch your ears.
- Push your arms forward like you were trying to close a heavy door.
- Tense your belly like you were trying to push out a poop.
- Squeeze your butt muscles like you were trying to hold in a poop.
- Tense your leg muscles by squeezing them together.
- Make a fist and squeeze your fingers and toes at the same time.

If you don't have time to tense and release each muscle group, you can tense your whole body at the same time or choose those muscles that you think need the most relaxing.

STEP 2: Figure Out Where the Stress Is Coming From
To figure out where your stress comes from, think about what frustrates you at home and school. Consider the things you have to do and the people you interact with during the day.

- Make a list of the things you don't like about school. Common things that bother kids are the amount of work, homework, a teacher's attitude and the difficulty of the work itself.
- If someone is bullying you, he may have threatened to hurt you or someone else if you tell anyone what's going on. You have to talk to a grownup if someone is picking on you. Bullies

almost never carry out their threats, but use them as a way to stop you from getting help.

- If the stress is coming from home, talk to your parents about it. If you can't talk to your parents, talk to a trusted teacher, coach, or doctor. These adults are trained to listen to kids and help them solve their problems.

STEP 3: Solve the Problem

Once you identify a stressful situation, you can begin to solve the problem. If you're having trouble with math, your parents can get a tutor or talk to your teacher to see if she can work with you before or after school. If you're having difficulty fitting in at school, your parents can arrange play dates on the weekend or ask the teacher to help you interact with your classmates. For example, you can sit at the same table or work together on a class project. If you're nervous about playing basketball because you miss lots of shots, your parents can arrange extra time at a gym or playground so you can practice until you feel more confident.

STEP 4: What If You Can't Solve the Problem?

Sometimes you won't be able to change a stressful situation, such as your family moving. If you spend all of your energy wishing the situation would change, your stomachache (or headache) will remain and may even get worse. The way to feel better is to choose something positive to focus on and try to get your thoughts to match the situation instead of fighting against it. For example, "I wish we weren't moving, but my mom gave me some tips for making new friends, and ways I can stay in touch with my old friends."

Happy Brain

STEP 5: Practice

It takes time to get the thinking part of your brain to take charge of the non-thinking part. In order to banish your Stress Monster, do the steps over and over even if they don't work right away.

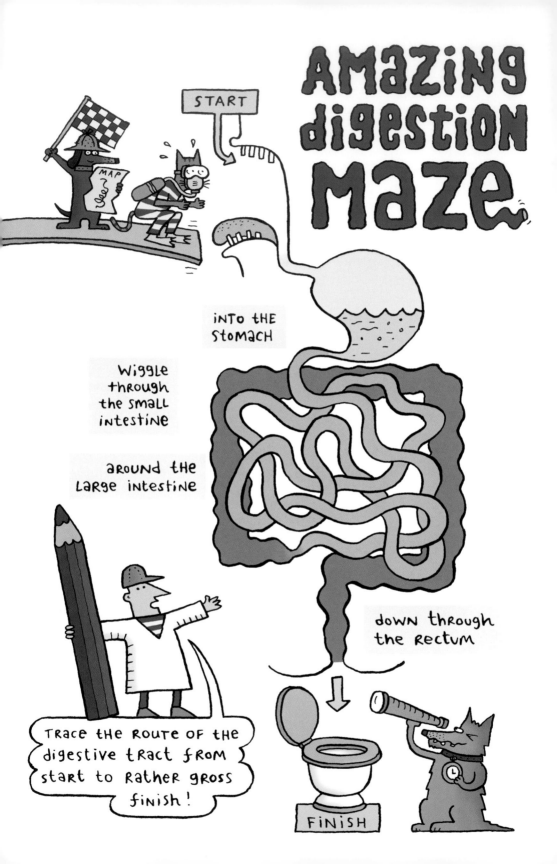

Lactose Unscramble

If you are lactose intolerant, you might want to avoid foods that contain milk or dairy products. Can you figure out the foods that contain lactose?

lmik
_____

cehtoacol kmil
_____

urogyt
_____

eechse
_____

izpza
_____

amc & sechee
_____

eic mcear
_____

cmrea hecees
_____

dipwhpe mcrea
_____

Laugh Out Loud!

Ever heard the expression "laughter is the best medicine"? Give it a try with these knock-knock jokes and riddles. See if you can make your parents laugh!

Knock Knock!
Who's there?
Iguana.
Iguana who?
Iguana hold your hand.

What word in the English language is *always* pronounced incorrectly?

Answer: Incorrectly.

Mary lives in a one-story yellow house. The couch is yellow. The chairs are yellow. The carpets are yellow. What color are the stairs?

Answer: Mary has no stairs. She lives in a one-story house.

Knock Knock!
Who's there?
Moo.
Moo, who?
Well, make up your mind.
Are you a cow or an owl?

If a rooster lays an egg on a flat surface, will the egg roll to one side or will it stay where it lands?

Answer: Neither. Roosters don't lay eggs, hens do.

Q&A ABOUT STOMACHACHES
(JUST foR PaReNTS!)

Stomachaches account for numerous visits to doctors' offices. Although serious disorders can cause abdominal pain (this is the term doctors prefer to describe stomachaches), the causes are usually due to something less worrisome.

Q *How common is abdominal pain in children?*

A Abdominal pain can broadly be divided into two types. Acute pain has been present for less than a week. Pediatricians see children with this type of pain every day. The problem is often caused by constipation, a viral infection, or even strep throat. Recurring pain occurs over a period of weeks, months, or years. Pediatricians see children with this type of pain a few times per week.

Q *What are the most common causes of recurring abdominal pain?*

A In a general pediatric practice, about 75% of recurrent abdominal pain is caused by lactose intolerance, constipation, or stress. Another culprit is diet, especially one that includes lots of foods with high-fructose corn syrup or corn syrup solids. Medicines like ibuprofen can also cause abdominal pain, though it occurs less often in children than adults.

Q *How does constipation cause abdominal pain?*

A Some children can have two bowel movements per week and experience no pain while others can pass one big poop per day and have lots of pain. Because many people do not understand how digestion works, they are unaware that fecal material can cause pain. That is why the book includes a detailed description of how the large intestine works.

Q *Is there a difference between nausea and pain?*

A This consideration is important when presenting information to your doctor. Abdominal pain and nausea are both uncomfortable, but they are not the same thing. Adults are good at distinguishing pain from nausea, but children may lump them together when describing how they feel. You can help them appreciate the difference by asking the following question: Does it hurt like you are being poked with a stick or do you feel like you might throw up?

Q *Is recurrent abdominal pain ever caused by anything serious?*

A Although uncommon in a general pediatric practice, serious medical disorders can present with recurring abdominal pain. The following diagnoses are ones doctors consider most often:

- celiac disease
- urinary tract infection
- Crohn's disease
- gastroesophageal reflux
- food allergies
- ulcerative colitis

Q *How do doctors diagnose recurrent abdominal pain?*

A When doctors see children with recurrent pain, they start with a detailed medical history because that often suggests a diagnosis. Pain that occurs more often during the week than on weekends or holidays is likely to have a stress component. Of course, weekends are not necessarily stress-free. Children may still have to deal with sports, or family issues such as parental separation or divorce.

Doctors often obtain blood, urine, and stool tests as well as an abdominal sonogram. In difficult cases, a child may be referred to a specialist for further evaluation.

Q *Are there clues that suggest the pain is due to a serious problem?*

A Although doctors are usually less concerned about recurring pain that is mild, the intensity of the pain does not always correlate with the diagnosis. The following symptoms increase the odds that a serious problem is causing the pain:

- If the child has recurrent vomiting or diarrhea, loses weight, or appears ill.
- If the pain awakens the child from sleep.
- If the pain is not located in the middle of the abdomen, i.e., around the belly button.

Q *Does medication help with recurrent abdominal pain?*

A Once the medical causes of pain have been eliminated, there are a number of interventions that can help. First, a well-balanced diet is always a good idea. Second, probiotics help some people with abdominal pain. A probiotic is a product that contains "good" bacteria. Because there are billions of non-harmful bacteria in your intestinal tract, taking probiotics has been shown to reduce pain. You should always talk to your doctor before taking any medication, including a probiotic.

One of the current thoughts about recurrent abdominal pain is that the child's nervous system is extra sensitive to the normal actions involved in the digestive process. The medical term for this is *visceral hyperalgesia.* (Viscera refers to the intestinal tract and algesia means sensitivity to pain.) There is evidence that certain prescription medications can help with this problem.

Answers

Lactose Unscramble

milk
chocolate milk
yogurt
cheese
pizza
mac & cheese
ice cream
cream cheese
whipped cream

About the Author

Howard J. Bennett, MD practices pediatrics in Washington, DC and lives in Maryland with his wife, two children, and three dogs. In addition to his books, Dr. B writes articles for the KidsPost section of the *Washington Post* and has a column in *Jack and Jill* magazine called "Life Is Gross." He is also the author of four Magination Press books:

Jessie MoJo Sadie

- *Harry Goes to the Hospital: A Story for Children About What It's Like to Be in the Hospital*

- *It Hurts When I Poop! A Story for Children Who Are Scared to Use the Potty*

- *Lions Aren't Scared of Shots: A Story for Children About Visiting the Doctor*

- *Max Archer, Kid Detective: The Case of the Wet Bed*

About the Illustrator

Spike Gerrell lives in North London with his partner Kaz, their son Ethan, daughter Stevie Jasmine, Freddie the cat, and a big load of stick insects. He likes cycling, running, making stuff and, of course, drawing. Most of all, though, he likes spending time with his kids.

FReddie the cat   STickie